THE GREAT DOG DISASTER

by Denise Ortman Pomeraning

illustrated by Don Robison

To my daughter Donna

Published by Willowisp Press, Inc.
401 E. Wilson Bridge Road, Worthington, Ohio 43085

Printed in the United States of America
10 9 8 7 6 5 4 3

ISBN 0-87406-406-6

Contents

Oh, No!
Not Again!

My dog Wizzer ran away again. He got out of the garage somehow. There's no way it was my fault.

But Mrs. Melby thought it was my fault that Wizzer got away. Mrs. Melby is my baby-sitter for after school when Mom and Dad are at work.

"Keegan, did that dumb mutt run away

again?" Mrs. Melby asked. "I asked you to keep the garage door closed."

"Wizzer is NOT a dumb mutt," I said. "He's a mixed-breed. He's smart. And I didn't open the garage door. He must have gotten out by himself."

Mrs. Melby looked at me.

"That door is big, Keegan," she said. "That door is heavy. It's electric. Your dog couldn't open it."

"But I didn't open it," I said.

"Then how could he get out?" she asked.

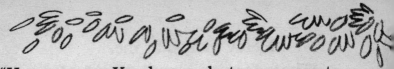

"He ran away. You know what your parents said about that."

"Oh, no," I said. My parents told me they might have to send Wizzer to the country if he ran away again. He would have to live with my aunt and uncle. I couldn't let that happen. Wizzer is the greatest dog in the world. Or, at least the greatest dog in our neighborhood.

I knew exactly what to do. There wasn't a moment to lose.

I ran over to Andy McMandy's house right away. Andy is my sometimes friend. He lives next door. I found him playing with his toy trucks in his backyard.

"Andy," I said, "you're well known in our neighborhood. You're a detective. I need your help. I'm accused of a crime I did not commit."

Andy McMandy
Takes the Case

Andy stopped playing with his trucks and stood up. He brushed his pants off and took his calculator from his pocket. Andy uses his calculator in his detective work. We hurried back to my garage.

"What's the crime?" Andy asked.

"Mrs. Melby thinks I'm the one who

opened the garage door," I answered.

"Why is that a crime?" asked Andy. "You don't need a detective. You need another baby-sitter." He started to leave.

"Wait!" I yelled. "I didn't open the garage

door. Wizzer escaped from the garage. But I don't know how he did it."

"Oh, I see," said Andy, holding his calculator up in front of him. "Maybe you do need a detective. Let's look at the facts. Your garage is attached to your house. The garage has three doors." He clicked the number three on his calculator.

"Door number one goes to the yard. Did he escape through that door?" Andy asked.

"No. It's always closed. When Wizzer gets into the yard, he steps on the flowers. And Mrs. Melby likes a neat garden."

"That's three doors less one," Andy said. He clicked the calculator again. "What about the door to the kitchen?"

"No," I said. "Mrs. Melby never lets Wizzer in the kitchen."

"That leaves the big door that goes to the driveway," said Andy.

"That door is electric," I said. "See that little brown box on the wall? It has a button on it. There's a little box inside the car that's just like it. If you push the button on the box, the garage door opens."

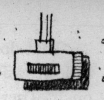

Crash!

Andy hurried over to push the button on the wall.

"Let me go first," I said. "It's my garage."

Andy put the calculator in his pocket. "Do you want me to take the case, or not?"

"Okay. But you can't reach it," I said.

"I've got an idea," Andy said. He dragged a trash can over to the wall and climbed up on it. "Here's how it's done," he said.

But when he stretched up to reach the button, his fingers missed it by a mile.

"We'll just make the pile a little higher," he said. "Bring me something to put on the trash can to make it higher."

I walked around the other side of my dad's car and got a sack of Wizzer's dog food. It was flabby and lumpy, but it was big. Wizzer eats a lot. He gets hungry from running around the neighborhood. I put the sack under Andy's feet.

He reached for the button again.

"This isn't hard at all," Andy said, grinning. But the sack slid as he pushed the button. The big door rumbled. The trash can tumbled. Crash! Andy landed in a cloud of dust. Old newspapers and empty boxes and chunks of dog food fell around him as he hit the floor.

Andy stood up and brushed himself off.

"Your dog couldn't have opened that garage door," he said. "It would take a giraffe to open it."

Mrs. Melby heard the crash and came running into the garage. "Now look what's happened!" she shouted. "I asked you not to open that door!" She grabbed a broom and began to clean up the mess.

Mrs. Melby likes a neat garage.

Where's Wizzer?

We got out of the garage as fast as we could. I looked around for Wizzer. I called his name, but he didn't come.

"That mutt made a fast getaway," Andy said. "But he didn't open the electric door."

"Wizzer's not a mutt, Andy," I said. "He's a mixed-breed. And if he didn't open the door, then who did?"

"Let's look at the facts again," Andy said.

"Someone very tall could reach that button. Or, someone very short," Andy added.
"It could have been someone short who is
a good jumper."

"Wizzer is a good jumper," I said.

"He's not that good," Andy insisted. "To
solve this case, we need to find someone
very tall or someone short who can jump."

Andy went on with the investigation. He walked around the garage and looked at his calculator.

"There are no fingerprints on the door," Andy said. "There are no footprints on the driveway." He clicked two zeros on his calculator.

"Mrs. Melby swept the driveway," I said.

The detective frowned. "Then she swept away the evidence," he said.

It was just my luck to have a baby-sitter who destroys evidence.

"Wait a minute," Andy said. He got down on his hands and knees. "Look over here, next to the driveway!"

"Those are paw prints," I said. "They head right across the street. Let's go!"

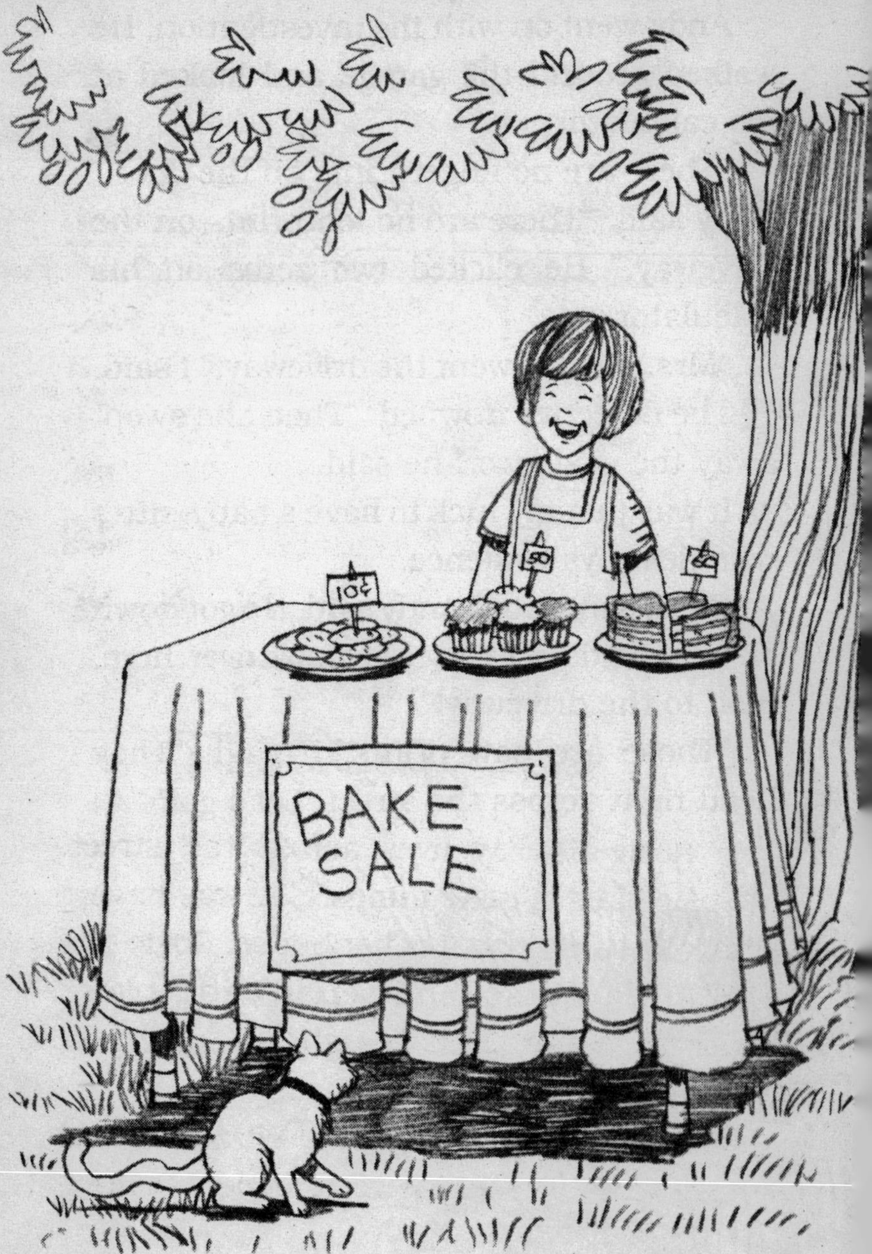
10¢
50
BAKE
SALE

What's an Accomplice?

Rosie Calotty lives across the street. Rosie likes to bake things. She was having a bake sale in front of her house. Rosie had all kinds of baked stuff set out on a table for people to buy. She thought we were customers. She was wrong.

"I'm looking for my dog, Wizzer," I told her. "Have you seen Wizzer, Rosie?" I asked.

"No," she answered. "I've been too busy trying to get kids to come to my bake sale."

"Well, we're not shopping," Andy said. He looked at Rosie carefully. Then he pulled me over to one side. He took out his calculator. "I'm figuring out how high it is from the garage floor to the button on the wall and how tall Rosie is."

I could tell just by looking at Rosie that she was too short to reach the brown box. But Andy figured it on his calculator, anyway.

"Rosie couldn't reach it," he said at last. "But she may have had an accomplice."

An accomplice? I didn't know what the word meant. So, I asked Andy.

"An accomplice is a person who helps a criminal commit a crime," said Andy.

"I don't think Rosie is a criminal," I said.

"She is a suspect," Andy said. "The paw prints led right to her yard."

Rosie called after us as we walked away, "The last time I had a bake sale, your dog ate all my cookies. Your mutt gives me a pain!"

Andy and I kept on walking.

"On second thought," I said, "maybe Rosie IS a suspect."

Follow the Paw Prints

The paw prints led through Rosie's yard to the muddy alley. Andy counted the prints on his calculator. Our shoes got heavy and sticky as we followed the clues. Mrs. Melby would have a fit when she saw my muddy shoes.

"Hurry, Andy," I said. "My mom and dad will be home from work pretty soon. Mrs.

Melby will tell them Wizzer ran away."

"So what if they find out?" Andy asked.

"They might send Wizzer to live in the country because he has run away so many times before. I just can't let them send him away." I got all choked up. I couldn't help myself.

"I don't like to tell you this, pal," said Andy. "But Wizzer is not popular in our neighborhood. He walks on flowers and eats cookies. And don't forget what he did to my calculator."

Oops. I had forgotten about that. One time Wizzer grabbed Andy's calculator off the table and ran away with it. We found it half-buried under a bush with some of Wizzer's bones.

"The calculator is still working, isn't it?" I asked. "You don't know Wizzer as well as I do, Andy. He's a great dog."

"But he couldn't open that electric door," Andy said.

"Who did open it then?" I asked.

"That's a very interesting question," said Andy.

Behind the
Wire Fence

The muddy paw prints led to a yard with
a wire fence around it. We could see a girl
with red hair jumping rope in the yard.

"There's Sarah Skinner," I whispered.

I told him about the time Wizzer wanted
to jump rope with Sarah. "Wizzer's tail and

feet got tangled in Sarah's jump rope," I explained. "They both fell down."

Andy looked carefully at Sarah. He clicked some numbers on his calculator.

Sarah didn't hear us or see us. She was jumping rope and counting aloud.

"As I was walking down the street, how many apples did I eat? One, two, three,

four..." she sang. She jumped all the way to 43 before she stopped for breath.

"Sarah," I called, "have you seen my dog? He has big paws, a happy face, and..."

"Don't forget his sloppy, wet, pink tongue," Sarah said. "Yes, I know your stupid dog, all right. He thinks he can jump

rope. He made me trip and fall. Your dog gives me a pain. I'm glad he ran away."

She began to jump again. "As I was walking down the street, how many bananas did I eat? One, two, three, four...."

"She could be more than just an accomplice," I said to Andy. "She could be IT." I kicked the fence in Sarah's yard. Some of the mud from my shoe came off on the fence. I was glad it did.

Has Wizzer Been Kidnapped?

"Sarah says Wizzer gives her a pain. Well, Sarah gives me a pain," I said, as we went on our way down the alley.

"Well, your dog did trip her and make her fall," said Andy. "Wizzer may have ruined her jumping record."

You can see why I call Andy a sometimes

friend. What a thing for him to say about Wizzer!

"Sarah Skinner thinks more of her old jump rope than she does of my pet," I said. "She'd let Wizzer out just to be mean."

"That's true," Andy said. "Maybe she

wanted revenge. And she's a good jumper. You know what I mean?"

I knew what Andy meant. He thought maybe Sarah could have jumped up and pushed the button. I also knew I wanted the mystery solved, and the sooner the better. I was more and more worried about Wizzer. Where had he gone? Would he come back? What if he had been hurt? Or lost? Or kidnapped?

"Andy, are you sure your calculator can help us find Wizzer?" I asked.

Andy didn't answer my question. He just looked at me. "Keegan, you asked me to take this case," he said. Then he added, "Besides, I think we're getting close to solving the case. I can just feel it."

Andy kept clicking in more and more numbers on his calculator. But I didn't think it was getting us any closer to finding Wizzer. And Mom and Dad would be home soon.

We came to the Double Bubble Car Wash at the end of the alley. "Wizzer wouldn't go past this place," I said. "He hates soap and water."

The trail was cold.

"Let's go back to the scene of the crime," Andy said.

I followed him. But I was starting to lose hope. Maybe Andy wasn't such a great detective, after all.

The Scene of the Crime

Andy and I walked slowly down the alley. We crossed the street to my house. I kept calling and calling for Wizzer. But he didn't come.

"I need a place to think and add up clues," Andy said when we got back to my house. "Thinking about crime makes me thirsty."

We went into the kitchen. It smelled like pine soap and floor wax.

"I'll say this for Mrs. Melby," said Andy. "She always keeps a good supply of pop on hand." I gave him a cherry pop.

Andy set his calculator on the table. The table was covered with things Mrs. Melby had cleaned that morning. There were bookends from the den, a blue jar, and a brown box.

"Be careful. If you spill pop on any of that stuff, Mrs. Melby might think I did that, too," I said.

Andy clicked some numbers on his calculator.

"This is one mystery that has to be solved fast, Andy. There's a lot at stake here," I said.

"Please don't rush me, Keegan," said Andy. "I'm thinking. Thinking takes time."

Andy's nose almost touched the calculator. "I'm adding paw prints and dividing them by the time it took us to get to the Double Bubble Car Wash. It took Wizzer the same amount of time as it took us to walk there. Maybe he was sniffing in garbage cans along the way."

While Andy mumbled on and on, I came up with a plan of my own. By then, I didn't care HOW Wizzer escaped. I just wanted to get Wizzer back.

I decided to put my plan into action. But right at that moment I heard the vacuum cleaner coming around the corner.

Mrs. Melby was at it again.

My Secret Plan

When I heard the vacuum cleaner, I got a little bit angry. My dog was gone. But Mrs. Melby doesn't care. She just goes right on cleaning.

"She wouldn't stop cleaning if an elephant got loose in the living room," I said. "She wouldn't stop cleaning if a volcano erupted in the backyard."

"Never mind that," Andy said. "Round

up the suspects. And hurry!"

This was the chance I needed. I had only a few minutes to get my plan ready.

First I went to get Rosie. A few cupcakes were left at her bake sale. I bought them, and the bake sale was over.

Then I went to get Sarah.

"Andy is going to hold a secret meeting at my house," I told the girls.

Rosie and Sarah love secrets. They reached my kitchen before I did. Before long the suspects were sitting around the table drinking cherry pop with the neighborhood detective.

"So, what's this secret meeting all about?" Rosie asked.

"Shhh." Andy held up his hand. "Here comes..."

All four of us were silent. We watched Mrs. Melby come in and put a tray on the table. Then she left the room.

"She collects things from all over the house just so she can clean them," I whispered. "She'll be back, so be careful what you say."

"Now here's the case," Andy said. "A dog escapcd this morning. Someone opened the garage door and let him out. What I want to find out, Rosie and Sarah, is WHO, HOW, and WHY."

"The dog may have opened the door himself," Rosie said.

"That's impossible. And you had a motive, Rosie," said Andy.

"Wait a minute, Andy," said Sarah. "Don't go using those detective words when we don't know what they mean. What's a motive?"

Andy looked at Sarah and shook his head. "A motive is the reason why a criminal commits a crime," Andy explained. "For

example, Rosie, the dog ate all the cupcakes at your last bake sale. You have a
motive for kidnapping him."

"Oh, brother," said Rosie. "You're nuts,
Andy."

"Wizzer's paw prints led to your yard,"
continued the detective. "And you were
close to the scene of the crime. You were
right across the street from it, to be exact."

Andy stopped talking when Mrs. Melby
came in to take away our empty pop cans.

"What about her?" Rosie asked in a low
voice as soon as Mrs. Melby left. "She can't
stand anything messy. Wizzer is the messiest dog in the neighborhood."

"He's the messiest dog in the universe,"
said Sarah.

"Mrs. Melby couldn't have done it," I
said. "She was inside cleaning. She even
dusted the TV while I was watching
Monster's Revenge."

"Be quiet, please. I have other evidence,"
Andy said. "Sarah, you are tall. It is a fact
that you could jump high enough to reach
the button on the garage wall that opens

the door." Andy clicked a few buttons on his calculator.

"But my house is at the end of the block," Sarah said. "I wasn't even near what you call the scene of the crime." Sarah and Rosie giggled.

Andy frowned. I could tell he didn't like them giggling at his detective work. "Maybe you wanted revenge," Andy said. "Remember, the dog ruined your jumping record. That's a..."

But he never got to finish what he was saying. We heard a sound. It was a loud bark that we all knew, and it was coming from outside. My secret plan had worked!

I got up and ran toward the sound. I bumped the table. Everything fell off the table. The bookends and the small brown box tumbled to the floor.

The small brown box was super-clean. It had a button on it. I grabbed it. I pushed the button and ran into the garage.

Rosie, Sarah, Mrs. Melby, and Andy followed me. They got to the garage just in time to watch the big door slowly rumble open. Wizzer strolled through the door.

When he saw me, Wizzer's tail began to wag around and around like the propeller on an airplane. He barked. He whimpered. He jumped all over me in excitement. He licked my face. I don't know who was happier, Wizzer or me.

The Case Is Closed

"The case of the mysterious escape is solved," I said.

Sarah dropped her jump rope.

Mrs. Melby dropped her dust cloth.

Rosie looked confused.

Andy frowned. "It's not solved yet," he said. "I'm still counting clues."

Sarah covered the calculator with her

hand. "Stop that crazy clicking, Andy," she said. "Keegan solved the case, not you."

"Tell us how your dog opened the door, Keegan," said Rosie.

"Wizzer didn't open the garage door," I said. "He's a smart dog, but he's not THAT smart."

I pointed at Mrs. Melby

and said, "She opened the door."

Everyone stared at Mrs. Melby, then at me, then at each other. Mrs. Melby's mouth fell open. But no words came out. Wizzer crept under the tool bench in the corner of the garage.

"It was you, Mrs. Melby," I said again. "You took the brown box out of the car. That box is the garage door opener. While you

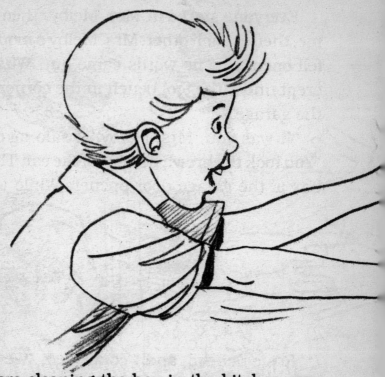

were cleaning the box in the kitchen, you touched the button. And bingo, the door opened. You didn't even know it happened. Wizzer saw the open door and walked out."

"But what made Wizzer come back?" Rosie asked.

"I did," I said. "I couldn't find Wizzer, so I made Wizzer find me. You know those cupcakes I bought at your sale, Rosie?"

Rosie nodded, and I continued, "Well, I left a trail of cupcake crumbs for Wizzer to follow. Wizzer ate his way right to the door. He barked when he got to the closed garage door." Just then Wizzer jumped up into my arms.

Andy turned off his calculator. He looked grumpy. I don't think Andy likes it when other people solve the neighborhood mysteries. But Mrs. Melby was laughing.

"This deserves a special treat," she said.

We went into the kitchen to watch Mrs. Melby. She took some lemonade out of the refrigerator. Then she took a big plate of chocolate-chip cookies off the counter.

"I just baked these," she said. "Come into the kitchen, and have a snack," she said. Then she looked down at Wizzer.

Wizzer looked up at her.

"All right, just this once," Mrs. Melby said.

Wizzer joined us in the kitchen. He went to his usual place, under the table. When Mrs. Melby wasn't looking, I gave Wizzer a big chocolate-chip cookie.

"I guess your dog's not so bad," said Rosie.

"He's nice, even if he is messy," added Sarah.

"I think I made a mistake on my calculator," said Andy. "That's why I couldn't solve the mystery as fast as you did, Keegan."

It was great to have my dog back again.

About the Author

DENISE ORTMAN POMERANING lives with her German shepherd, Travis, in Colorado Springs, Colorado. When she's not writing about Keegan and Andy and Wizzer, she writes for the local newspaper in Colorado Springs. She also likes hiking in the Rocky Mountains, going on picnics, and watching parades.

Once when Denise was helping her daughter clean house, something happened. The dog got out of the garage in exactly the same way Wizzer does in *The Great Dog Disaster*. "I didn't have a neighborhood detective like Andy McMandy to help me find him," says Denise. "So, I had to figure it out for myself."